Princesses Don't Wear THAT!

WRITTEN BY

CAT WHITE

 FriesenPress

Suite 300 - 990 Fort St
Victoria, BC, V8V 3K2
Canada

www.friesenpress.com

ISBN
978-1-03-910337-5 (Hardcover)
978-1-03-910336-8 (Paperback)
978-1-03-910338-2 (eBook)

1. JUVENILE FICTION, CLOTHING & DRESS

Distributed to the trade by The Ingram Book Company

TO MY DAD, who has always said,

"There's no such thing as bad weather, just bad clothing."

AND TO MY OWN TWO POWERFUL PRINCESSES—

try to embrace glitter and grit in equal measure. I'm discovering

the balance makes life much more fun and meaningful.

There is a special white cat

with grey spots who loves

Nora and her room.

Can you spot the cat
in the book?

Nora was a princess—

or at least she thought she was a princess. Every day she

wore beautiful, sparkly pink, purple, or golden dresses.

She liked to twirl and whirl and dance around while

pretending she was at a fancy ball in her very own castle.

NO OTHER CLOTHES WOULD DO FOR PRINCESS NORA.
ONLY PRETTY PRINCESS DRESSES.

But outside, the air was getting cooler and the leaves were turning red, orange, and yellow. The sound of gusty wind filled the air.

One crisp autumn day, Nora's mom said,
"Nora, it's time to put on PANTS, A WARM SWEATER, AND RUNNING SHOES. We're going to the park."

Nora didn't like that idea one bit.

"PRINCESSES DON'T WEAR THAT!" SHE CRIED. "PRINCESSES ONLY WEAR PRETTY DRESSES."

"Oh, really?" asked her mom. "Will you have fun in the wind if you're wearing your princess dress? The wind might blow your dress everywhere,

the crunchy leaves will get in your shoes and between your toes,

and you could

get stuck
in a tree

while building a

fairy village with the

Forest Princess."

Nora thought about it for a moment.

She wanted to have fun at the park.

"Well," she sighed, "I GUESS I COULD PUT ON
MY PANTS, A WARM SWEATER, AND RUNNING SHOES."

And off they went to the park in the

right clothes for the right occasion.

The days grew shorter and the trees became bare.
The sound of crunching footsteps through the
snow filled the air.

One cold winter's day, Nora's mom said,
"Nora, it's time to put on your SNOWSUIT, BOOTS,
MITTENS, AND HAT. We're going outside to play."

Nora didn't like that idea one bit.

"PRINCESSES DON'T WEAR THAT!" SHE CRIED.
"PRINCESSES ONLY WEAR PRETTY DRESSES."

"Oh, really?" asked her mom. "Will you have fun in the snow if you're wearing your princess dress? You might get very cold building your snowman,

yummy snowflakes won't be able to land on your tongue through your chattering teeth,

and your dress

could freeze
like an icicle

when you visit the

Snow Princess in her

magical ice castle."

Nora thought about it for a moment.

She wanted to have fun outside.

"Well," she sighed, "I GUESS I COULD WEAR MY SNOWSUIT, BOOTS, MITTENS, AND HAT."

And off they went to play outside in the

right clothes for the right occasion.

The snow eventually melted and green grass began to peek through. The sound of chirping birds filled the air.

One rainy spring day, Nora's mom said, "Nora, it's time to put on your RAINCOAT, PANTS, AND RAIN BOOTS, AND GRAB YOUR UMBRELLA. We're going outside to do some gardening."

Nora didn't like that idea one bit.

"PRINCESSES DON'T WEAR THAT!" SHE CRIED. "PRINCESSES ONLY WEAR PRETTY DRESSES."

"Oh, really?" asked her mom. "Will you have fun in the rain if you're wearing your princess dress? You might get **very soggy** as you jump into lake-sized puddles,

rain drops will land
directly on
your nose,

and you could get

super muddy

when you plant a

secret garden with the

Flower Princess."

Nora thought about it for a moment.

She wanted to have fun in the garden.

"Well," she sighed, "I GUESS I COULD WEAR
MY RAINCOAT, PANTS, AND RAIN BOOTS,
AND TAKE MY UMBRELLA."

And off they went to the garden in the

right clothes for the right occasion.

The days grew warmer and the sun shone bright. The sound of children playing and laughing filled the air.

One hot summer's day, Nora's mom said, "Nora, it's time to put on your SWIMSUIT, HAT, SANDALS, AND SUNSCREEN. We're going to the beach."

Nora didn't like that idea one bit.

"PRINCESSES DON'T WEAR THAT!" SHE CRIED. "PRINCESSES ONLY WEAR PRETTY DRESSES."

"Oh, really?" asked her mom. "Will you have fun in the sun if you're wearing your princess dress? You might get all hot and sweaty when you build the world's largest sandcastle,

your popsicle will melt all over your dress and ruin it,

and your dress

could get

tangled
up in the
seaweed

when you swim

with the beautiful

Sea Princess."

Nora thought about it for a moment.

She wanted to have fun at the beach.

"Well," she sighed, "I GUESS I COULD WEAR MY SWIMSUIT, HAT, SANDALS, AND SUNSCREEN."

And off they went to the beach in the
right clothes for the right occasion.

And then, a very special day arrived. The sound of an excited young girl filled the air.

Nora's mom said, "NORA, IT'S TIME TO PUT ON YOUR DRESS. We're going to your birthday party!"

Like every time before, Nora started saying,

"PRINCESSES DON'T WEAR . . . WAIT . . .

She stopped with a surprised look on her face.

"WHAT DID YOU SAY?"

"That's right," her mom said.

"OF COURSE PRINCESSES WEAR PRETTY DRESSES ON THEIR BIRTHDAY!

How else will you have fun at your tea party in the park, enjoy your delicious birthday cake, and laugh and play with your princess friends?"

Nora smiled the biggest smile she could smile.

The right clothes for the right occasion, she thought to herself as she pulled on her sparkly pink and purple princess dress and shiny shoes.

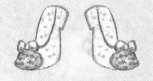

AND OFF THEY WENT TO HER

FANCY PRINCESS TEA PARTY.

Acknowledgements

Immeasurable love and thanks to my biggest cheerleader and husband, Jon. Your patience and support for this journey has made all the difference in the world.

Thank you to Adora Nwofor, Kunji Ikeda and Jennie Vallis for your cultural sensitivity consultations on my illustrations. Your insights have taught me how me how to be a better ally through accuracy, representation, and inclusion.

If you love Nora and her adventures, also

look for the second book in this series called

Princesses Can Be WHAT?

This book encourages young readers to dream

about their future, beyond the princess dress.

About the Author

Cat White holds a master's degree in Outdoor Environmental and Sustainability Education. While teaching young children in an outdoor setting early in her career, she experienced the ways in which appropriate attire benefits imagination and play.

Her first picture book, PRINCESSES DON'T WEAR THAT!, was inspired by her own daughter's love of dresses and the challenge of getting her to wear anything else. Cat lives in Calgary, Alberta, with her husband, Jon, and two young daughters. Her girls are free to embrace the glamour of princess play and encouraged to get dirty in the mud!

CPSIA information can be obtained
at www.ICGtesting.com
Printed in the USA
LVHW071344051021
699577LV00022B/931